This book is not dedicated to my agent, Steven Malk.

It's dedicated to his wisdom and most excellent guidance over the years.

—R.D.S.

To Moony

—C.E.

Text copyright © 2022 by Randall de Sève
Jacket art and interior illustrations copyright © 2022 by Carson Ellis

Visit us on the Web! rhcbooks.com
Educators and librarians, for a variety of teaching tools, visit us at RHTeachersLibrarians.com

Library of Congress Cataloging-in-Publication Data
Names: de Seve, Randall, author. | Ellis, Carson, illustrator.
Title: This story is not about a kitten / by Randall de Seve ; illustrated by Carson Ellis.
Description: First edition. | New York : Random House Studio, 2022. | Audience: Ages 4–8.
Summary: A neighborhood comes together to help a kitten without a home.
Identifiers: LCCN 2021048001 (print) | LCCN 2021048002 (ebook) | ISBN 978-0-593-37453-5 (hardcover) |
ISBN 978-0-593-37454-2 (lib. bdg.) | ISBN 978-0-593-37455-9 (ebook)
Subjects: CYAC: Cats—Fiction. | Animals—Infancy—Fiction. | Neighbors—Fiction.
Helpfulness—Fiction. | LCGFT: Picture books.
Classification: LCC PZ7.D4504 Th 2022 (print) | LCC PZ7.D4504 (ebook) | DDC [E]—dc23

The text of this book is set in 16-point Eaves Century Modern.
The illustrations in this book were rendered in gouache.
Interior design by Rachael Cole

MANUFACTURED IN CHINA
10 9 8 7 6 5 4 3 2 1
First Edition

THIS STORY IS NOT ABOUT A KITTEN

written by Randall de Sève

illustrated by Carson Ellis

RANDOM HOUSE STUDIO ▲ NEW YORK

This story is not about a kitten.

A kitten, hungry and dirty,
scared and alone,
meowing sadly,
needing a home.

This story is not about the dog

who stopped when it heard the kitten,

hungry and dirty,

scared and alone,

meowing sadly,

needing a home.

This story is not about the
dog's people who listened,
or the dog who stopped
when it heard the kitten,
hungry and dirty,
scared and alone,
meowing sadly,
needing a home.

This story is not about the

woman who held the dog

for the dog's people who listened,

or the dog who stopped

when it heard the kitten,

hungry and dirty,

scared and alone,

meowing sadly,

needing a home.

This story is not about the twins
who brought a box,
or the woman who held the dog
for the dog's people who listened,
or the dog who stopped when it

heard the kitten,
hungry and dirty,
scared and alone,
meowing sadly,
needing a home.

This story is not about the man drinking tea

who offered some milk,

or the twins who brought a box,

or the woman who held the dog

who stopped,

or the dog's people who listened

and quietly . . .

carefully . . .

coaxed the kitten

who clawed
and hissed
and fought a big fight

until . . .

"We'll call her Amber," everyone agreed.
But who could take her home?

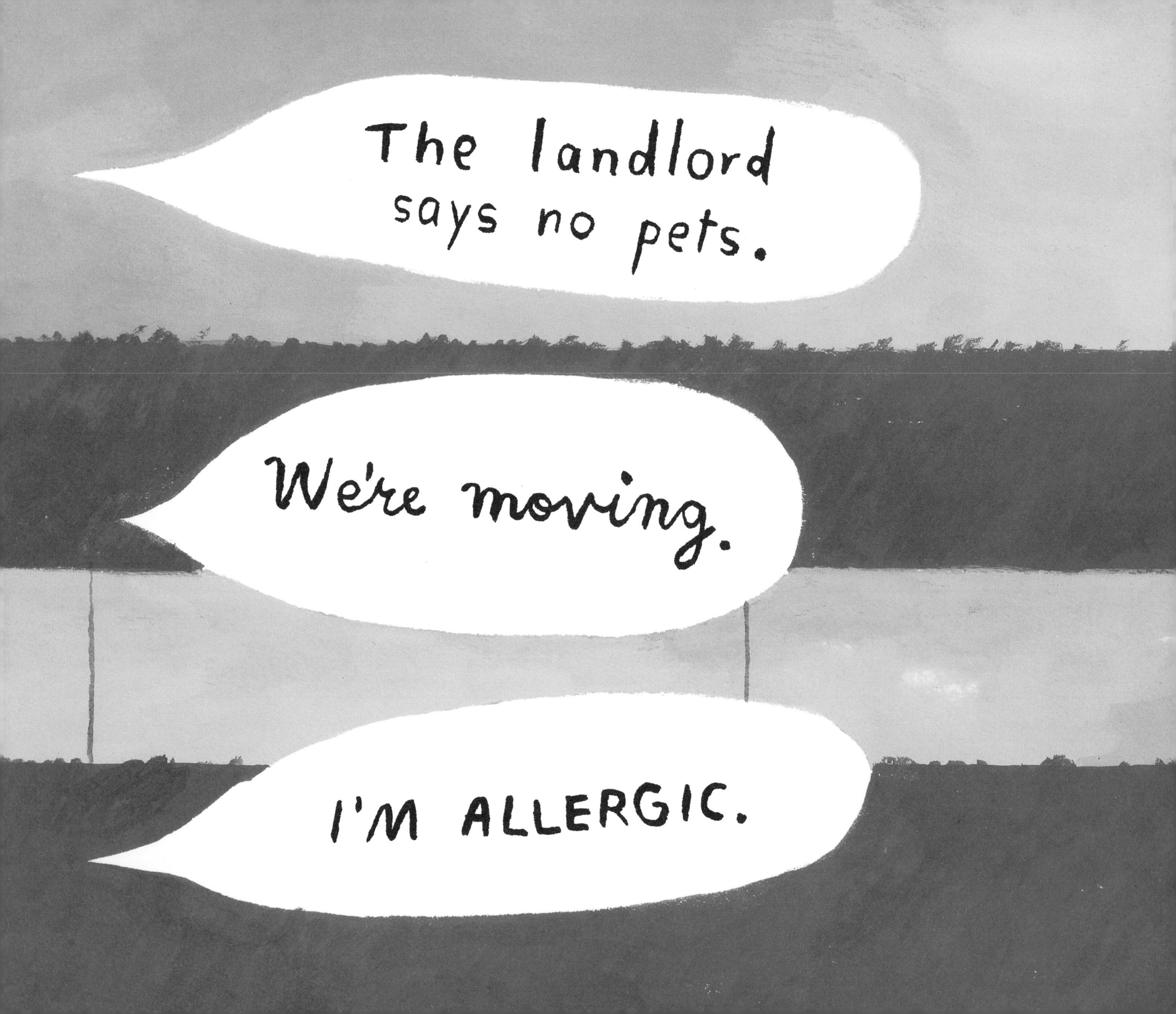
The landlord says no pets.
We're moving.
I'M ALLERGIC.

This story is not about the child who asked, "Could we?"

or the man who offered some milk,

or the twins who brought a box,

or the woman who held the dog

for the dog's people who listened,

or the dog who stopped when it heard the kitten—

now full-bellied and clean,

no longer alone,

purring happily.

Home.

This story is about the
stopping
and listening,
the holding
and bringing,
the offering
and asking
and *working together*
it takes, sometimes, to get there.

Amber is the sweetest.
Can I visit her every day?
YUP.
Achoo!
GESUNDHEIT!